MARVEL
AVENGERS

BATTLE AGAINST THE BLACK ORDER

AUTUMN PUBLISHING

CRRAACK! A massive sound jolted through Avengers Tower, where Shuri and T'Challa were showing Doctor Bruce Banner some Wakandan tech they were working on.

"What was that?" asked Shuri.

"It wasn't thunder, that's for sure," said Banner. "Let's check it out."

The heroes burst out onto the roof and stopped dead in their tracks. "Whoa," Shuri said. "I was not expecting that."

"Proxima Midnight!" cried Banner. He had heard tales of the Super Villain, one of Thanos' strongest allies, throughout the years. "What is she doing on Earth?"

"Give me a hand and I'll explain later!" Captain Marvel called out. But Shuri's gauntlets weren't ready yet.

Shuri ran back to the lab in Avengers Tower to fix her gauntlets. Banner turned into the Hulk and followed T'Challa into the fight.

WHACK! Proxima Midnight immediately attacked Black Panther, but Hulk responded by knocking her towards the edge of the roof!

"HULK SMASH!" Black Panther called out. He looked excited. "I've always wanted to say that."

The heroes watched Proxima as she soared through the air.
"No, wait!" cried Captain Marvel, as she dived after her.
Even though Proxima was fighting her friends, Captain Marvel needed to find out what Proxima was doing on Earth in the first place.
But before Captain Marvel could reach her, the Super Villain disappeared into thin air.

Captain Marvel flew back to the roof, where the other Avengers were waiting.

"There were two members of the Black Order coming to Earth: Proxima and Corvus Glaive," Captain Marvel said. "Corvus got away while I was chasing Proxima. I don't know where he is now."

"Why do you think they're here?" Black Panther asked.

Captain Marvel shook her head. "All I know is that if Thanos sent them, they're up to no good."

Suddenly, Banner got an incoming distress call from Ant-Man! Ant-Man's face filled the screen. "Banner! Help!"

"That's Corvus Glaive's weapon," Captain Marvel said urgently, watching the tiny hero dodge and dash away from the glinting blade.

"Look," Banner said, pointing at the map. "We have to get to the waterfront!"

"I'll catch up!" Shuri called from the lab. "As soon as I get these gauntlets working..."

"Hurry, Sister!" Black Panther urged her on.

Scott Lang, known as Ant-Man, was having some super-bad luck.
He'd been minding his own business when this weird-looking space
demon attacked him out of nowhere!

"Boy, am I glad to see you!" cried Ant-Man to the arriving Avengers.
"Who is this guy?"

"Corvus Glaive," said Captain Marvel. "One of Thanos' pawns. What I don't know is why he's after you."

"I can answer that," Corvus said. "Thanos wants Ant-Man because he wants to know how Pym Particles work."

Pym Particles were responsible for giving Ant-Man his powers to grow and shrink. In the hands of Thanos, the particles could be catastrophic.

"Well, Thanos isn't finding that out today," Captain Marvel said.

"What Thanos wants, Thanos gets," Corvus Glaive said dismissively.

Even fighting four Super Heroes at once, Corvus was proving unstoppable. No matter how hard the heroes came at him, he wouldn't go down.

BAM! Black Panther landed a surprise kick, bringing Corvus to his knees, at which point Captain Marvel discharged a knock-out blow.

"Follow my lead!" Black Panther called to Captain Marvel.

Corvus was still standing, but barely.
"I think we got him!" Ant-Man cried. "No Pym Particles for you, pal!"
But just as Hulk was about to deliver the finishing touch...

... Proxima Midnight reappeared! "Oh geez," Ant-Man said, shaking his head in disbelief. "There's another one?!"

"You were barely able to handle one of us," Proxima gloated. "How can you fight us both?"

"I was wondering that myself," Ant-Man said, as the rest of the heroes gathered to protect him.

Without the whole team in place, the heroes had their hands full!

Black Panther sailed towards Captain Marvel after a rough blow from Corvus.

"I feel like we could really use Shuri and those new-and-improved blasters right about now," Captain Marvel said.

"Um... guys? Over here?" Ant-Man gave a nervous chuckle as he struggled against Proxima.

Any moment, she would teleport away with him and Thanos would have the secret of Pym Particles!

POW! Shuri appeared out of nowhere and knocked Proxima flying with an energy punch from her updated gauntlets.

Ant-Man was set free!

"She hits like the Hulk!" Captain Marvel said.

With Shuri's tech, the Super Heroes quickly gained the upper hand.
"Better late than never!" Black Panther called out to his sister.
Shuri laughed. "The combination of Wakandan and Stark tech is unbeatable!"

"We've failed him, Corvus," Proxima called out to her ally. "Abort mission!"

Before the heroes could catch them, Proxima and Corvus teleported away.

"Whew," Ant-Man said. "That was too close."

"Piece of cake," Shuri said. "All we had to do was get the whole team together."